One Hundred
Wishes

by Enid Richemont and Ben Whitehouse

W

FRANKLIN WATTS
LONDON•SYDNEY

Old Stan lived all alone in a grim, grey house.

He put high fences all round his garden,

with huge signs saying: KEEP OUT!

Everyone thought he was grumpy,

so nobody visited him and he had no friends.

Every night, he sat on his own,

just counting his money.

"I don't need any friends," said Stan.

"All I need is my money."

One day, a fairy godmother
knocked on Stan's front door.
"Who are you?" said Stan.
"What do you want?"
"I'm **your** fairy godmother," said the
fairy godmother. "Can I come in?
I'm here to give you three wishes."

Stan thought about what to wish for.

Perhaps he could ask for a guard dog
to bark and keep people away?

Or a higher fence so that people could not see
into his garden?

Maybe he could ask for some more money
to count?

Suddenly he had an idea.

"Here's my first wish," he said.

"I wish for three more wishes."

His fairy godmother frowned.

"Oh, alright then," she said,

and three more wishes appeared.

"Only five wishes?" thought Stan, counting.

"I want a lot more than that!"

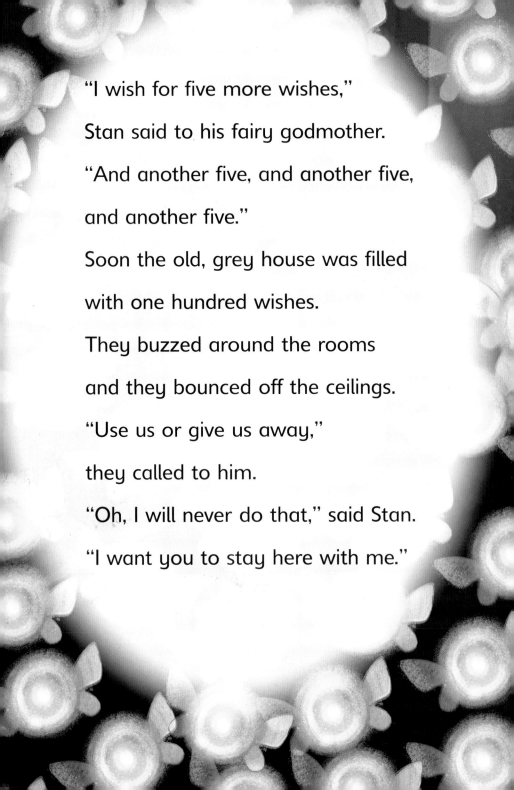

"I wish for five more wishes,"
Stan said to his fairy godmother.
"And another five, and another five,
and another five."
Soon the old, grey house was filled
with one hundred wishes.
They buzzed around the rooms
and they bounced off the ceilings.
"Use us or give us away,"
they called to him.
"Oh, I will never do that," said Stan.
"I want you to stay here with me."

9

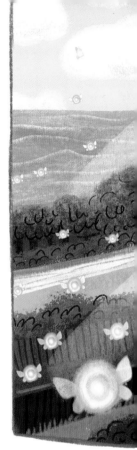

Then, one morning, BANG!

Stan's bedroom window blew open,

and the wishes rushed outside.

"Use us, or give us away," they called.

"Don't go," cried Stan, but only one wish

came back. The rest of the wishes were free.

Some flew over trees and fields.

Some flew over mountains and over the sea.

Three flew up the street, and three flew down.

The wishes got to work.

"I wish for a fish,"

thought the cat at Number One.

"I wish for a stick,"

thought the dog at Number Two.

"I wish I could be an astronaut,"

thought the girl at Number Three.

"I wish my bike still worked,"

thought the boy at Number Four.

"I wish my back didn't hurt,"

thought the old woman at Number Five.

"I wish I could pay the bills,"

thought the man at Number Six.

Later that day, the fairy godmother flew in through Stan's open window.

"Your wishes have done well," she said.

"And it's all thanks to you."

"But those wishes were MINE," grumbled Stan.

"I wanted them to stay with me."

Stan's fairy godmother frowned again.

"Remember what they said:

Use us or give us away," she said.

"You still have one wish left.

Remember, you must use it well."

Stan thought hard. Then he went pink.

"I wish, I wish ... it's a secret."

Stan whispered his wish.

The wish disappeared and an invitation

fluttered down.

The fairy godmother picked it up.

"There's going to be a street party

this afternoon," she said. "You're invited."

"But I've never been to a party,"

muttered Stan.

The fairy godmother shook her head.

"Well you have to go to this one," she said,

"or you won't get your wish."

Street Party
This Saturday
Bring Something
to Share!

Everyone had to bring something to share
at the party.

"I haven't got anything to share," thought Stan.

Suddenly, a huge iced cake appeared.

"You can't eat that all by yourself,"

said the fairy godmother, with a smile.

17

Lots of people came over to talk to Stan.

"Nice things have been happening," they said,

"and we think it's something to do with you."

People shook his hand. People hugged him.

Stan couldn't stop smiling.

"That was my wish," he whispered

to his fairy godmother.

"To have some friends."

"Well, your wish came true!"

smiled his fairy godmother.

19

Story order

Look at these 5 pictures and captions.
Put the pictures in the right order
to retell the story.

1

The wishes came true for Stan's neighbours.

2

The wishes escaped.

3

Stan made friends at the party.

4

Stan lived all alone and had no friends.

5

A fairy godmother granted Stan three wishes.

Independent Reading

This series is designed to provide an opportunity for your child to read on their own. These notes are written for you to help your child choose a book and to read it independently.

In school, your child's teacher will often be using reading books which have been banded to support the process of learning to read. Use the book band colour your child is reading in school to help you make a good choice. *One Hundred Wishes* is a good choice for children reading at Gold Band in their classroom to read independently.

The aim of independent reading is to read this book with ease, so that your child enjoys the story and relates it to their own experiences.

About the book

Stan lives all alone in his grim, grey house. Nobody talks to him because they think he is so grumpy. Then a fairy godmother appears and grants him some wishes. Stan's life is about to change!

Before reading

Help your child to learn how to make good choices by asking: "Why did you choose this book? Why do you think you will enjoy it?" Look at the cover together and ask: "What do you think the story will be about?" Ask your child to think of what they already know about fairy godmothers and wishes. Ask: "Do you think the man will be making one hundred wishes?"

Remind your child that they can sound out the letters to make a word if they get stuck.

Decide together whether your child will read the story independently or read it aloud to you.

During reading

Remind your child of what they know and what they can do independently. If reading aloud, support your child if they hesitate or ask for help by telling the word. If reading to themselves, remind your child that they can come and ask for your help if stuck.

After reading

Support comprehension by asking your child to tell you about the story. Use the story order puzzle to encourage your child to retell the story in the right sequence, in their own words. The correct sequence can be found on the next page.

Help your child think about the messages in the book that go beyond the story and ask: "Do you think that Stan was happy at the beginning of the story? Why/why not?"

Give your child a chance to respond to the story: "If you could make just one wish, what would it be?"

Extending learning

Help your child reflect on the story, by asking: "Stan was lonely at the beginning of the story. Have you ever felt like that? What could you do to feel better if you feel lonely?"

In the classroom, your child's teacher may be teaching different kinds of sentences. There are many examples in this book that you could look at with your child, including statements, commands and questions. Find these together and point out how the end punctuation can help us decide what kind of sentence it is.

Franklin Watts
First published in Great Britain in 2018
by The Watts Publishing Group

Copyright © The Watts Publishing Group 2018
All rights reserved.

Series Editors: Jackie Hamley and Melanie Palmer
Series Advisors: Dr Sue Bodman and Glen Franklin
Series Designer: Peter Scoulding

A CIP catalogue record for this book is
available from the British Library.

ISBN 978 1 4451 6259 1 (hbk)
ISBN 978 1 4451 6261 4 (pbk)
ISBN 978 1 4451 6260 7 (library ebook)

Printed in China

Franklin Watts
An imprint of
Hachette Children's Group
Part of The Watts Publishing Group
Carmelite House
50 Victoria Embankment
London EC4Y 0DZ

An Hachette UK Company
www.hachette.co.uk

www.franklinwatts.co.uk

For David Richemont, star-gazer – E.R.

FSC
www.fsc.org
MIX
Paper from
responsible sources
FSC® C104740

Answer to Story order: 4, 5, 2, 1, 3